MY NEW YORK

KATHY JAKOBSEN

Little, Brown and Company
Boston   Toronto   London

In memory of my good friends
Jay Johnson and Bob Bishop

The paintings in this book are oil on canvas.

First Edition

Library of Congress Cataloging-in-Publication Data
Jakobsen, Kathy.
    My New York / Kathy Jakobsen. — 1st ed.
        p.   cm.
    Summary: Becky, a young New Yorker, takes the reader and a friend
from the Midwest on a tour of her favorite places in the city.
    ISBN 0-316-45653-5
    1. New York (N.Y.) — Description — 1981– — Views — Juvenile literature.
2. New York (N.Y.) in art — Juvenile literature.
[1. New York (N.Y.)]   I. Title.
F128.37.J34   1993
974.7'1'00222 — dc20   91-33567

10 9 8 7 6 5 4 3 2 1

SC

Published simultaneously in Canada by Little, Brown & Company (Canada) Limited

Printed in Hong Kong

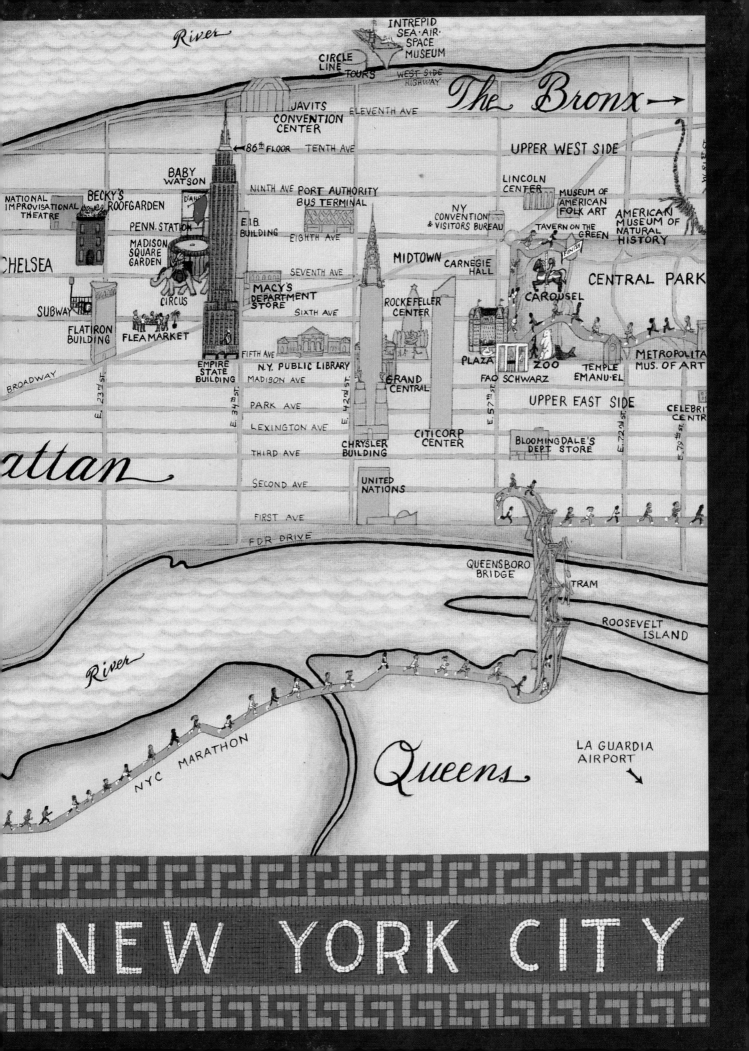

LOOKING SOUTH FROM CENTRAL PARK

THE ROOF OF MY APARTMENT BUILDING

𝒟ear Martin:

I'm excited you're going to move here! I miss you and the Midwest and can't wait to show you all around New York. Here are some of my favorite places. I'm in all of them—see if you can find me. I drew a map for you, too. We can follow it when you get here.

*R*ight around the corner from where I live in Chelsea is the Sixth Avenue Flea Market. It has lots of neat stuff. I go there almost every Saturday, especially if my friend Bob is going to be there. He saves me the best baseball cards. The sidewalks

here look like a jungle because it's the flower district. The Sixth Avenue subway runs right below. You can feel the trains rumbling by right under your feet.

In New York, the streets are busy—above ground and underground, too, where there are subway tunnels, steam pipes, water mains, natural gas and electric lines, and more than eleven million miles of telephone wires! Some of the city's early

UNDERGROUND

water pipes were just hollow logs. Today, someone is always digging up the streets. My dad says that's how they keep things fixed and the city running.

THE EMPIRE STATE BUILDING

We don't have any really tall buildings in Chelsea, where I live, but wait until you see the Empire State Building. It's 102 stories high! It's the same building we saw in that old King Kong movie, remember? When I stand at the bottom and look up, I feel like an ant, but when I'm at the top and looking down, it's the people on the streets below who look like ants!

*I*f you want to see some real ants, I'll take you to the Central Park Zoo. The tropical rain forest exhibit has over 100,000 leaf-cutter ants (they're behind glass)—plus bats and red-bellied piranhas. It gets pretty steamy in there, so I like to cool off afterward in the Polar Circle. The polar bears and penguins swim so close, you can

CENTRAL PARK ZOO

almost touch them. Gus, the largest polar bear, weighs seven hundred pounds!
For a special treat on hot days, he and the other bears get apples frozen in round
ice blocks.

FRIEDSAM MEMORIAL CAROUSEL

*N*ot far from the zoo is the carousel. I've named my favorite horse Fritz. There's a dappled gray horse I know you'll like. Just across the street from the park is F.A.O. Schwarz. They have a zoo of stuffed animals—including polar bears that look just like Gus in the Central Park Zoo.

OPPOSITE: F.A.O. SCHWARZ

Across the street, near the Plaza Hotel, we can visit my friend Victor and his horse, Cuddy. Victor's a carriage driver. Some of the carriage horses wear rubber horseshoes to protect their feet from the pavement. It's just like wearing sneakers!

THE PLAZA HOTEL AND CENTRAL PARK

There's always something happening on this corner. Once we watched a film crew shoot a movie. During the holidays, we always come up here to look at the decorations and buy hot roasted chestnuts from the street vendors.

THE NEW YORK CITY MARATHON

$\mathcal{E}$very year, more than 25,000 people from all over the world run in the New York City Marathon. The route covers all five boroughs of the city. This year, I handed out water to the runners on the corner of First Avenue and Fifty-ninth Street. When I'm eighteen, I'll be able to run in it myself.

CHINATOWN

Chinatown isn't far from the Stock Exchange, where my mom works. Sometimes, for a special treat, my dad and I meet her here for dinner. Do you know how to use chopsticks? If not, I'll show you. And then after, we can walk to Bayard Street to get ice cream made from red beans!

My favorite dessert is Baby Watson cheesecake. Mario D'Aiuto makes it. He's been in the bakery business for over forty years, and every box of his cheesecake has his baby picture on it. He has so many customers now that he uses over 38,000 eggs a day! His original building is small and always crowded.

We like to take a long walk after we stop for cheesecake. There are always new buildings going up all around the city. I like to watch the construction—especially when they dynamite or the big cranes are operating.

OPPOSITE: A BUILDING GOING UP!

BELOW: THE HOME OF BABY WATSON CHEESECAKE

WILDERNESS THAT CAN REVEAL
ITS MYSTERY ITS MELANCHOLY
AND ITS CHARM

THE NATION BEHAVES WELL IF IT
TREATS THE NATURAL RESOURCES
AS ASSETS WHICH IT MUST TURN
OVER TO THE NEXT GENERATION
INCREASED AND NOT IMPAIRED
IN VALUE

CONSERVATION MEANS DEVELOPMENT
AS MUCH AS IT DOES PROTECTION

THEODORE ROOSEVELT

THE AMERICAN MUSEUM OF NATURAL HISTORY

*O*n a rainy day my favorite place to visit is the American Museum of Natural
History. You won't believe how big the dinosaurs are—the barosaurus is fifty feet
high and longer than a city bus!

$\mathcal{W}$hen you're here, you'll be able to go to the circus at Madison Square Garden. Spring in New York means the circus is in town! Once when we were at Baby

Watson's, we watched the elephants parade right down the street on their way
to the circus train.

THE *INTREPID*

On the Hudson River, we can visit a real aircraft carrier called the *Intrepid*. My great-uncle Frank was stationed on it during World War II. Now it's the Sea-Air-Space Museum. I like to pretend I'm the pilot of one of the Douglas Phantom Fighters parked on deck. We can also climb around in the USS *Growler*, which is right nearby—it's the world's only guided missile submarine open to the public.

THE SOUTH STREET SEAPORT

*N*ew York doesn't have skyscrapers everywhere. Visiting the South Street Seaport is like stepping back in time. In the old days, there were so many ships here that their masts looked like a forest. My favorite tall ship that's docked here is the *Peking.* It's longer than a football field and has masts seventeen stories high.

One of the best views of New York is from the Staten Island Ferry. It's a good way to see the Statue of Liberty and Ellis Island, too. When my great-grandfather Sigward came from Norway, the Statue of Liberty was probably the very first thing he saw of America. When you're here, we'll climb to the top. She's so big that forty people can stand inside her head.

NEW YORK HARBOR

You'll get here just in time for the Fourth of July fireworks! They're set off in New York Harbor not far from the Statue of Liberty. It's a real thrill. I can't wait to see them—and you!

OVERLEAF: THE FOURTH OF JULY

K Jakobsen ©1986

COAST GUARD

31

MY FRIEND MARTIN

$\mathcal{B}$ye for now!
Your friend,
Becky

P.S. Be sure to bring your sneakers — we're going to be doing a lot of exploring!